# KNIGHTMARE

For Lucy, Theo and Tara – PB

STRIPES PUBLISHING
An imprint of Little Tiger Press
1 The Coda Centre, 189 Munster Road,
London SW6 6AW

A paperback original
First published in Great Britain in 2015

ISBN: 978-1-84715-644-0

A CIP catalogue record for this book is available from
the British Library.

Printed and bound in the UK.

10 9 8 7 6 5 4 3 2 1

# KNIGHTMARE
## A Dog's Life!

PETER BENTLY

**stripes**

# CEDRIC'S WORLD

## CASTLE BOMBAST

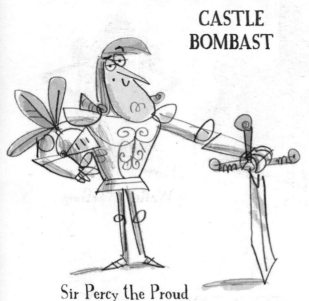

Sir Percy the Proud

Cedric
Thatchbottom
(Me!)

Patchcoat the Jester

Margaret the Cook

# BLACKSTONE FORT

Walter Warthog

Sir Roland the Rotten

# SPIFFINGTON MANOR

Algernon Whympleigh

Sir Spencer the Splendid

# Chapter One
## Royal Request

SNIP!

"Ouch! Careful, Cedric! You're not supposed to cut off the whole dashed toe."

"Sorry, Sir Percy."

Clutching my master's left foot in one hand and a pair of scissors in the other, I had another go at trimming the little toenail.

"How's that, Sir Percy?"

# KNIGHTMARE

My master put down his spoon, stroked his stubbly chin and peered at his toenails. "Hmm. *Almost* there, Cedric. Just a smidgen more off the big toe. That should do the trick."

# KNIGHTMARE

"Yes, Sir Percy."

He settled himself back on the pillows and scooped up another mouthful of his porridge. I stifled a sigh and snipped again.

A large yellowish sliver of toenail nearly hit me in the eye. Before I could see where it landed, I heard hooves clattering in the courtyard.

"Ah, that'll be the post, Cedric. Off you go."

"Yes, Sir Percy."

I ran down to the castle courtyard to greet the rider. I expected it to be a regular messenger with the post, but it was one of the king's heralds, looking rather bewildered.

"Good morning," he said. "I'm trying to find Castle Bombast, but I think I must be lost."

"No, you're not," I said. "This *is* Castle Bombast."

"Really?" said the herald. "As in Sir Percy the Proud's place?"

"Yes," I replied. "I'm Sir Percy's squire."

"Oh," the herald said. He seemed taken aback. "Break time is it?"

"I beg your pardon?"

"Or perhaps they're all out on patrol."

"Er, *who* are?" What *was* the herald going on about?

"The castle garrison," said the herald. "At the palace they told me Castle Bombast

10

is 'crawling with guards'. So I was a bit surprised to ride in without being challenged. Thought I'd got the wrong castle."

"Um – well…"

Castle Bombast "crawling with guards"? I don't know where he'd got that idea from. Sir Percy couldn't afford any proper guards. The castle's security was basically me making sure I locked the front gate every night.

"Anyway, I can't hang about chatting," the herald went on. "Give this to your master." He thrust a sealed scroll into my hand, turned his horse and rode off out of the gate. The seal bore the king's coat of arms.

I hurried back up to Sir Percy's bedchamber, waving the scroll. "Urgent letter, Sir Percy," I said. "From the king!"

Sir Percy sat up.

"The king?" he said. "How splendid! Perhaps it's to do with that survey he sent out last week to all his knights. Do you remember, Cedric?"

"Oh yes," I said. "His Majesty wanted to check that everyone's looking after their castle properly. In case there's ever a war. You replied by the next post."

"Indeed," said Sir Percy. "I expect His Majesty wishes to thank me for answering so swiftly. Kindly read me the letter."

I tore open the seal and started to read.

12

Dear Sir Percy,

Thanks for your reply to my survey. Well, well. I'm simply amazed at your improvements to security. So Castle Bombast is now crawling with guards, eh? And you've got a highly trained guard dog, too. Excellent! The last time I visited, the castle was about as secure as a wet paper bag.

I agree, it definitely does sound a **LOT** better than Sir Roland's castle. Which means I've got just the job for you. I've ordered a **TOP SECRET** weapon for my army. A platoon of royal troops, led by my Chief Herald, Baron Fitztightly, is on its way to collect it from the makers. They'll need to stop overnight on the way back to the palace. Somewhere ultra-safe and secure. Castle Bombast is the ideal place! The baron will be arriving early tomorrow evening.

Fredbert R.

P.S. If anything happens to my new weapon it's the dungeons for you. Toodle pip!

Now I understood what the messenger had been going on about! I looked at my master. He had a rather dazed expression on his face.

"I think the king must be mistaken," I said. "You didn't *really* say we had loads of guards, did you, Sir Percy? Or a guard dog?"

"Good gracious no, Cedric!" he spluttered. "That is to say, I mean, er, I suppose I *may* have hinted that my garrison was – um – a *tad* bigger than is currently the case. After all, one doesn't want to, er, *disappoint* one's monarch and all that."

My heart sank. Sir Percy had been boasting again. And this time he'd really landed himself in it.

"I shall simply write back to His Majesty at once and explain that it's all been a misunderstanding," he went on. "By fast post the letter should reach him tonight. When did he say the baron was arriving? Tomorrow?"

"Yes, Sir Percy," I said. "But it was *yesterday's* tomorrow, if you see what I mean. The baron's arriving today. He's already on his way."

"Aargh!" Sir Percy whimpered, burrowing under his pillow. "What are we going to do, Cedric?"

Uh-oh. That "we" spelled trouble. Luckily, I had an idea.

# KNIGHTMARE

"How about borrowing some guards off
Sir Spencer?"

Sir Spencer was Sir Percy's best friend
and his castle was fairly close by. He didn't
have many guards, but they would be
better than none at all.

Sir Percy sat up again. He looked
aghast. "Good grief, no!" he said.
"Borrowing another knight's guards? The
humiliation! Spencer would never let me
live it down. You'll have to come up with
a better plan than that, Cedric."

"Er, *me*, Sir Percy?"

"Yes, Cedric," Sir Percy said. "All you
have to do is make the baron believe this
is a fantastically fortified stronghold.

# KNIGHTMARE

I'm sure you'll think of something. It's only for one night, after all. Consider it part of your knight training. It'll be the perfect preparation for when you're – um – er, under siege."

"Yes, Sir Percy," I said, trying to sound convinced.

"That's the spirit!" my master beamed. "I'm relying on you, Cedric. If the baron twigs that the castle has no guards, he'll tell the king and I shall be *seriously* in the doghouse. Which reminds me. It's not just *guards* we need."

"Isn't it, Sir Percy?"

"Indeed not," he replied. "We need a guard dog."

"A dog, Sir Percy?"

"Precisely, Cedric."

"But where will you get a dog from before this evening, Sir Percy?"

"Oh, *I* shan't be getting one from anywhere, dear boy," said my master. "*You* will. I remember Sir Spencer once purchased a very fine greyhound from a place near Stoke Bluster. You'd better go there immediately. After you've laid out my best tunic, of course. And my razor. Oh, and the new aftershave that I bought off that travelling apothecary."

"Yes, Sir Percy."

"Just this once I suppose I shall have to get dressed by myself," my master sighed.

"As soon as I've finished my breakfast."

As he scooped up the last dollop of porridge, I noticed something sticking out of the spoon. I opened my mouth to warn him, but it was too late. He downed the spoonful in one gulp.

Toenail and all.

# Chapter Two
## Kennel Kerfuffle

"A *dog*? Just another bloomin' mouth to feed, if you ask me."

Margaret the cook was *not* happy to learn that Sir Percy would have unexpected guests that evening. She was even less happy when I told her about Sir Percy needing a guard dog.

"An' where's this mutt going to sleep, Master Cedric?" she grumbled, waggling a half-plucked starling in my direction. "Not in my kitchen, that's for certain. It'll eat everything in sight!"

"That'll teach it," chuckled Patchcoat the jester, who was building a house of cards on the kitchen table.

Margaret glowered at him. "I 'eard that, Master Patchcoat," she said. "Any more o' your cheek and it's no starling stew fer you."

"Ooh, is that a promise?"

Patchcoat ducked quickly to dodge a swipe from Margaret's half-plucked bird.

"I'm serious," said Margaret. "There's little enough food to go round as it is, what with the world and 'is wife turnin' up out of the blue."

I would hardly have called Baron
Fitztightly and a platoon of the king's own
soldiers "the world and his wife", but I kept
that to myself. I had bigger things to worry
about. Like how to convince the baron that
Castle Bombast was crawling with guards.

Getting a guard dog was a start, but we still needed some actual *guards*.

"Hmm. Tricky one, Ced," said Patchcoat when I explained the problem. "Tell you what, I'll have a think about it while you're out buying this guard dog."

"Thanks, Patchcoat."

"No probs. And by the way, where do you find a dog with no legs?"

"Um – I've no idea," I said.

Patchcoat grinned. "Exactly where you left it. See ya, Ced!"

As I walked along the lane to Stoke Bluster, I seriously began to think Sir Percy must

23

have got the wrong place. For half an hour I hadn't seen a single human, never mind a dog. But then I spotted two merchants coming towards me on a pony cart piled high with rugs and blankets. It was a pretty warm day, but they were both wearing scarves and hats pulled down over their eyes.

# KNIGHTMARE

"Excuse me," said one of the men, who was poring over what looked like a map. "Tell me, is this the way to Castle Bombast?"

"Yes," I said. "Straight on then next left and just keep going. But—"

I was about to add that I worked at Castle Bombast and that we didn't need any extra rugs, thanks, but the driver had already flicked the reins and started to ride on.

The lane was barely wide enough for the cart to pass down it. I was just wondering why they hadn't taken the main road when I spotted a sign in the hedge, half hidden by leaves.

25

**SIMNEL OF STOKE BLUSTER**
**PREMIER POOCHES**
**DOG BREEDER TO THE GENTRY**
**HIGH-CLASS HOUNDS**
**TIP-TOP TERRIERS**
**SUPER-DUPER SPANIELS**
**ROBBER-GOBBLING GUARD DOGS**
½ Mile This Way →

I followed the sign and, sure enough,
I soon came to a tidy-looking farmhouse
next to a yard full of kennels. Tied up
outside were dozens of dogs of different
shapes and sizes.

# KNIGHTMARE

A man in an apron came out of the farmhouse carrying a bucket of meaty mush with a few large bones poking out. The dogs all sat up smartly and wagged their tails.

"Master Simnel?" I said.

"That's me, sonny," said the man. "Can I help you?"

"My master's sent me to buy a dog."

"A dog, eh?" said Simnel. "You've come to the right place. All my dogs are trained to the highest standards. Watch this." Simnel nodded to a well groomed spaniel. "Fifi, hup!"

Fifi jumped into the air and turned a perfect backwards somersault.

"Good girl," said Simnel proudly,
ladling an extra dollop of dog food into the
spaniel's bowl.

"Impressive!" I said. "But my master's
actually looking for a *guard* dog. Do you
have something a bit … bigger?"

# KNIGHTMARE

"Ah, I see," said Simnel. "Perhaps something like Sir Roland? Follow me!"

As Simnel led the way across the yard, I smiled at the idea of some mutt being named after Sir Percy's arch-rival. But when I saw the dog, I couldn't have thought of a better name. Sir Roland was a huge mastiff with a thick spiked collar. He was almost as tall as me. And he definitely had more muscles.

"'Ere you go, Roly," smiled Simnel, giving the mastiff a huge bone out of the bucket. "'E's a big softie, isn't you, Roly dear?"

Sir Roland crunched the bone in two with a single bite and eyed me with a look that said "dessert". Simnel patted his head and scratched him behind his ears. "One of my best, is Roly," he said. "Any knight would be glad to have him. A snip at ten shillings."

*Ten shillings!* Yikes, that was expensive. It was then that I realized Sir Percy hadn't given me any cash at all. I tipped my money pouch into my hand. A few measly coins fell out.

# KNIGHTMARE

"That all you've got?" frowned Simnel. "For a pedigree guard dog? Is your master having a laugh?"

"Er..."

"WOOF!"

I just had time to glimpse a brown shape hurtling through the gate before I was knocked flat on my back.

Then a woman's voice shrieked, "Come 'ere, you no-good, sausage-eatin' fleabag!"

The next thing I knew I was being licked by a large slobbery tongue.

"Aargh! Gerroff! Help!"

The tongue belonged to a big, gangly, goofy-looking dog.

"Sorry 'bout that, lad," said Simnel. He grabbed the chewed stump of rope attached to the dog's collar and pulled the pooch off me. A plump woman came puffing up. She wagged a stubby finger at Simnel.

"Chewed through his lead again!" she scolded. "Then he sniffed out a whole string o' sausages in the cupboard. That's the third lot this week. *And* I had them in a box where I thought he couldn't find 'em. Husband, I ain't puttin' up with it no more. Either this useless mutt goes or *I* do."

She strode off into the farmhouse.

There didn't seem much point hanging around any longer. I didn't have enough money to buy a guard dog and that was that.

"Oh well," I said, getting to my feet. "I'd better be going. Sorry to waste your time, Master Simnel."

"Hold on, sonny," said Simnel, as I turned

to leave. "I suppose I do have *one* dog you might be able to afford."

"Really?" I said. "Where?"

He nodded at the animal sitting at his feet, his tongue lolling daftly out of the side of his mouth.

"Hercules here."

"Er, and he's definitely a *pedigree* dog?" I asked.

Whatever breed Hercules was, it wasn't one I recognized. He had the wiry fur of a terrier, the long lolloping legs of a wolfhound, and the floppy ears of a retriever. And, if his gormless grin was anything to go by, the brains of a pigeon.

"Well," said Simnel. "He's er, a – a

terrier-retriever-hound. Egyptian. Yes, that's it."

"An *Egyptian terrier-retriever-hound?*" I said. "I've never heard of one of those before."

"Er, let's just say that he's the first of his breed," said Simnel. "Which is why I'm offerin' him at the special price of … sixpence."

I counted the coins in my fist. "I've only got tuppence ha'penny," I said. "Sorry."

"That'll do," said Simnel, swiping the coins. "He's all yours. You've got yourself a bargain there, sonny! He may not be much to look at, but he's got an amazing sense of smell. Oh, just one thing. He hates aniseed.

You know, that stuff they use to make liquorice."

"But I thought all dogs loved aniseed?"

"Not this one. Fell in a vat of the stuff as a puppy. It's the only thing that drives him round the bend. Anyway, I'd better finish feedin' the dogs. Good luck!"

He handed me the stump of rope and strode off. I had just bought a dog.

# Chapter Three
## Cellar Snoop

I led Hercules back to Castle Bombast.
Or rather, Hercules led *me*. When he wasn't
barking gleefully at fields of cows and
sheep, the pesky pooch kept dragging me
off to chase birds, or to give passers-by a
great slobbery greeting. And when there
were no sheep, cows, birds or people to run
after, Hercules stopped to sniff out some

new scent he'd discovered. That's when he wasn't cocking his leg on just about every tree in sight.

It was lunchtime when we finally got back to the castle. Patchcoat was practising some juggling in the courtyard.

"Whoops!" he cried, as one of the balls he was juggling came flying our way. Hercules barked with glee, sprang free from my grip and snatched it from the air. To my horror he instantly chewed it to bits and swallowed it in one gulp.

"Bad dog!" I cried, running up and grabbing Hercules by the rope. "I'm really sorry, Patchcoat. I'll get you another ball."

Patchcoat laughed. "Don't worry, Ced.
It was only a stale roll I found in the
kitchen," he said. "Good catch, boy!"

Hercules jumped up and gave Patchcoat
a soggy lick. "Well, he's a big chap all
right," he said, ruffling the dog's head.
"But don't you think he's a bit *friendly* for a
guard dog?"

"I know," I agreed, struggling to keep
a tight grip on Hercules's rope. "But he's
all I could afford. Did you think of any
bright ideas to make the castle look well-
guarded?"

Patchcoat shook his head. "Sorry."

"What about hiring a few soldiers?" I
said. But then I sighed. "No, that's no good.

It would mean getting money out of Sir Percy."

"Yeah," chuckled Patchcoat. "Which is about as likely as sailing across the world without falling off the edge. At this rate we'll have to dress up as guards ourselves."

"Actually, Patchcoat, that's not a bad idea," I said. "If the baron sees two guards standing at the gate with Hercules, he might not notice that the rest of the castle isn't guarded."

"D'you know, that could just work, Ced. But we'd have to look the part or the baron might recognize us."

It was true. We'd met Baron Fitztightly several times before.

# KNIGHTMARE

"So we'd need proper uniforms," I sighed. "Helmets and chain mail and stuff."

"We could try the castle cellars," said Patchcoat.

"Really?" I said. "Isn't it just a big empty room?"

"Nah. There's tons of old junk down there, just wait and see," said Patchcoat.

We headed into the castle. The cellar door was just off the Great Hall, right next to the kitchen. While Patchcoat popped in for a candle, I waited outside the door with Hercules. The pooch snuffled and scratched at the door, but I didn't dare let him in with Margaret about. I was relieved when Patchcoat came out with a lighted candle.

# KNIGHTMARE

A flight of stone steps led from the cellar door down into a large, bare and chilly chamber. When Sir Percy had visitors, this was where their servants slept. There was nothing in the room apart from a dozen straw mattresses, which I kept neatly made up with old pillows and blankets. So I was NOT pleased when Hercules pounced on one of the mattresses, grabbed a pillow in his jaws and started to shake it madly.

"No, Hercules!" I said, trying to pull it out of his mouth. But he just held on even tighter, growling playfully.

"Reckon he likes a game of tug of war, Ced!" said Patchcoat. "Just make sure you don't pull too hard or—"

# KNIGHTMARE

RRIIIIPPP!

The pillow burst in an explosion of feathers. They filled the room and covered absolutely everything.

"*Atishoo!* Bad dog!" I said. "Now I'll have to clear up before the baron's soldiers sleep here tonight."

# KNIGHTMARE

As Hercules merrily shook the last of
the feathers out of the wrecked pillow,
Patchcoat pointed to an old door.

"Through here," he said. "After you, Ced!"

"Really?" I said. "I always thought that
was just an empty cupboard."

I opened the door, which creaked on its
rusty hinges. I held tight to Hercules's rope
as he stuck his head in and sniffed around.
To my surprise I saw that it led into
another chamber.

"Ugh!" I said, brushing a cobweb out of
my face.

"Welcome to the oldest part of Castle
Bombast!" said Patchcoat.

I tried to ignore the squeaks and

scuttling sounds that greeted us. The vast, gloomy chamber seemed to be full of junk. In the candlelight I could just about make out old tables and chairs with legs missing, empty barrels, threadbare tapestries and rugs, and chests of cracked crockery. Patchcoat spotted a dusty old candlestick and stuck the candle in it.

"Blimey!" I said, dodging a startled bat. "Some of this stuff looks ancient."

"Probably is," said Patchcoat. "The cellars are all that's left of the original castle. Sir Percy's ancestor built it hundreds of years ago. Sir Pancras the Preposterous his name was."

"There's a painting of him in the Great Hall," I said. "He's the one dressed as a chicken."

We picked our way through the junk.

"How much further do the chambers go on for?" I wondered.

"Under the entire castle," said Patchcoat. "There's even supposed to be a secret passage down here somewhere. But that's probably just an old tale."

CLANG!

"Ouch!" I'd just stubbed my toe on something hard. I bent down to rub it and saw a pile of rusty old helmets and mailcoats. "Hey, look!" I exclaimed. "Perfect guard costumes!"

"Excellent!" said Patchcoat. "And I've just spied some old spears and battleaxes. They're a bit rusty but basically all right."

Suddenly Hercules gave a yelp of delight and shot ahead, almost yanking my arm out of its socket in the process. He was heading for something against the far wall. In the dim light it looked like a line of soldiers.

47

# KNIGHTMARE

"Calm down, Hercules," I laughed. "It's just a bunch of old jousting dummies, you dummy."

The dummies were made of painted canvas stuffed with mouldy old straw. The stuffing was coming out of them where they'd been hit during lancing practice. (Obviously not by Sir Percy. My master couldn't hit a barn door if it was right in front of his nose.) Hercules merrily sniffed the dummies and widdled on one or two for good measure.

"They did look real from a distance," I said. "Especially in the dark…"

Patchcoat grinned. We stared at each other, then at the dummies, then at the pile of old mailcoats and weapons.

"Hmm," I said. "Patchcoat, are you thinking what I'm thinking?"

"You bet, Ced!"

"It'll probably never work," I said. "But anything's worth a try. Come on, let's get this stuff out of the cellar."

## Chapter Four
### Training Trouble

Our plan was to dress the dummies as soldiers and hope that the baron would believe there were a dozen guards up on the battlements. It would be getting dark when he arrived, so he might just fall for it.

It took us nearly an hour to haul all the chain mail, helmets, spears and the dummies up on to the castle battlements. As I staggered up the steps under a heap of heavy helmets, one of them slipped off and clattered down to the courtyard below.

A window opened above us. "Cedric, do keep the noise down, will you?" It was Sir Percy, blinking in the afternoon sunshine. "I was just in the middle of a – um – some, er, very important business." He rubbed his eyes and stifled a rather obvious yawn.

*Ah yes*, I thought. *The very important business of having a nap.*

"Sorry, Sir Percy," I said.

Then Sir Percy spotted Patchcoat scratching Hercules's tummy.

"I say, whose dog is that?"

"*Yours*, Sir Percy," I said. "His name's Hercules. He's an Egyptian terrier-retriever-hound. Actually I had to pay for him myself, so do you think—"

"Ah, splendid, splendid!" my master interrupted. "Looks like a fine specimen. Good work, Cedric. Now I simply must get ready for the baron. Where did you put my razor and aftershave?"

# KNIGHTMARE

"On the table in your chamber, Sir Percy," I said. Something told me I wasn't going to get my money back any time soon.

"Excellent. Carry on, Cedric. But quietly, please!"

He shut the window and we went back to our task. As Patchcoat lugged the last of the dummies from the cellar, I spotted something trailing out of a box of ancient books. To my surprise, it was an old dog lead.

"Perfect!" I said. "Hold still, Hercules."

I undid the stump of rope and tossed it into the junk. While I was putting on the lead I glanced at some of the books. Most were musty manuals with worm-

eaten covers and titles like *Are You Sitting
Comfortably? Garderobes Through the
Ages* and *Pigging Out: Wild Boar Recipes
of the Rich and Famous*. Then something
caught my eye.

Just the thing! I tucked the book
under my arm and headed outside after
Patchcoat.

# KNIGHTMARE

"Look what I found," I said. "It might give me a few tips on how to make Hercules more convincing as a guard dog."

"Looks a bit *dog-eared* to me," Patchcoat said with a grin.

I groaned. "Look, you start dressing up the dummies. I'll come and give you a hand in a bit. I'm off to train Hercules."

"Righto, Ced. Oh, and what's the difference between a knight and a warm dog?"

"No idea," I said.

"The knight wears armour. The dog just pants. Cheerio!"

# KNIGHTMARE

I tied Hercules to an apple tree in the garden and sat down beside him with the book.

I flicked through the yellowed parchment pages. There was some interesting stuff about tracker dogs in Chapter Four, but it was Chapter Five that really got my attention.

### Training A Guard Dog

"The simple act of chasing a stick," I read, "is excellent practice for pursuing burglars, peasants and other undesirables."

I found a good-sized stick then untied Hercules's lead and put it in my pocket. He was eagerly sniffing the air.

I threw the stick across the garden and hollered, "Good boy! After it!"

# KNIGHTMARE

Hercules shot off – in completely the wrong direction.

"Stop!" I called. "Come back, you daft dog!"

I might as well have been shouting at the tree. I sprinted after him and managed to grab his collar, but stumbled on a fallen apple. Before I knew it, the manic mutt had yanked me off my feet and was towing me across the grass towards... Yikes!

SPLAT!

"Urghh!" I yelled, as Hercules charged straight through Grunge the gardener's compost heap. I let go of his collar and heaved myself out of the stinky, steaming pile. Brushing off the worst of the muck,

I spotted the dog in the turnip patch. He was digging furiously with his massive paws, scattering earth all over the place.

"Stop it!" I cried, ducking as Hercules sent a muddy turnip whizzing past my ear. "Bad dog! Grunge'll kill me!"

Hercules suddenly stopped digging and emerged from the hole with an old sheep bone in his jaws.

"Blimey," I gasped. "D'you mean you could actually smell that bone from over there?"

But I didn't stay impressed for long. The door of the nearby hut opened and Grunge shuffled out carrying a spade. I hastily stepped in front of the hole.

# KNIGHTMARE

"Afternoon, Master Cedric," he croaked. "'Ere, what's that animal doin'?"

"Oh, er, n-nothing!" I stammered. "It's Sir Percy's new guard dog. I'm trying to train it, you see…"

"Well, train it somewhere else," Grunge grumbled. "Margaret says we got extra guests for dinner. I needs to dig up another turnip."

"Er, I know!" I fibbed. "Look, I've saved you the bother!" I picked up a stray turnip and handed it to Grunge. "Here you go."

"Righto. Thank 'ee, Master Cedric." Grunge took the turnip and shuffled off.

I kicked the earth back into the hole as best I could and reattached Hercules's lead.

"Right, you hairy horror," I said. "I think we'd better continue our training well away from the castle."

We made our way across the castle grounds towards Sir Percy's woods. Plenty of sticks there, I thought. And *no* turnips or manure heaps.

# KNIGHTMARE

Hercules totally ignored the first few sticks. But then I threw another and he gave a WOOF! of delight and sped after it.

*At last he's got the hang of it*, I thought. But when Hercules reached the stick and carried on running, I realized it wasn't the stick he was chasing at all but a rabbit. I watched in dismay as the bolting bunny scarpered into the trees and Hercules disappeared after it.

"Stop!" I hollered, starting to run. "Hercules! Here, boy! Come back!"

Hercules was already out of sight among the trees. I called his name but it was no use. He could be anywhere. As I stopped for breath, I heard a twig cracking. I peered through the trees and bushes. There seemed to be two people up ahead.

"Hello!" I called hopefully. "Have you seen a dog?"

There was no reply, and when I went to look the figures had vanished. I thought I must have been mistaken. But then I spotted something shiny on the ground. A coin! When I bent to pick it up I realized there were fresh footprints, too. So I *had* seen someone. The coin looked foreign, but it was definitely silver and I guessed it must be worth a shilling or two.

As I slipped it in my pocket, I heard a woman cry out, "Hey! What's that dog doing?"

# KNIGHTMARE

I headed for the voice and came to a
clearing. In the centre stood a colourful
caravan. A horse was grazing nearby. Beside
the caravan stood a man and woman,
both wearing headscarves, large earrings
and bright, exotic clothes. The woman was
holding Hercules firmly by his collar.

"This your dog, dearie?" she said.

"Yes! Thank you!" I said. "How on earth did you catch him?"

"Easy," she said. "He stopped for a widdle on our cart wheel."

"Oh," I blushed. "Sorry about that."

"No harm done," said the man, who was holding a short plank of wood. "But you ought to keep him under control. Not much good as a *poacher's* dog if he won't obey you." He winked.

"Eh?" I said. "But I'm not a poacher."

The pair laughed.

"Very funny," said the man. "Don't worry, we won't let on. We glimpsed your mates in the wood but they hid as soon as

we came near. And you look like you've
been sleeping outdoors for a week."

"An' you *smell* like it an' all," said the
woman. "No offence, dearie."

"Look, I'm really *not* a poacher," I said.
"I had, er, a bit of a collision with a compost
heap, that's all. I work for Sir Percy up at
the castle. These are his woods. And he'll
certainly be interested to know that there
are trespassers about."

The man and woman exchanged
worried looks.

"Oh, I didn't mean you," I said. "I meant
those poachers you spotted. I'm pretty sure
I saw them, too. I think they dropped this."

I held up the coin.

"Phew," said the woman, relieved. "Y'see, some folks don't like havin' us gypsies around."

"Don't worry," I said. "I won't tell Sir Percy you're staying here."

"Thank you, young master," the woman said. "I'm Rosie, by the way."

"An' I'm Jed," said the man. "Is there anythin' we can do for you in return?"

Rosie pulled a polished glass sphere out of her pocket. "I can tell you your fortune, if you like, dearie," she said, peering into the ball. "Hold on... I can see a couple of mysterious strangers headin' your way..."

"Er, no thanks," I said. I remembered that I'd come across Rosie before. She'd

been telling fortunes at the May Fair.
While Rosie was staring into her ball, Jed
took out a length of rope with knots in it
and started measuring the plank of wood
he was holding.

"Are you a carpenter?" I asked.

"Yup," said Jed. "I'm just mendin' a hole in
the caravan floor. You want somethin' fixin'?"

I thought for a moment.

"Actually, I do need somewhere for
Hercules to sleep. Any chance you could
knock up a kennel before tonight?"

"Easy!" said Jed. "Plenty of wood
around here, after all! I'll bring it to the
castle later. Who shall I ask for?"

"Cedric." I smiled. "Thanks, that would
be brilliant. Here, you can have this as
payment. It's probably not enough but it's
all I've got." I handed Jed the silver coin.

"Thank 'ee, Master Cedric," he said.
"That'll do nicely."

Rosie was still staring into her crystal
ball. "Ooh!" she declared. "Well I never!
I can see a man flying!"

"Really?" said Jed. "Who is it?"

# KNIGHTMARE

"Dunno. He's dressed like a knight or summat. Oh! He's just landed in a river! At least, I *think* it's a river…"

I glanced at the ball. "I can't see anything," I said.

"Ah, that's coz you ain't got the *gift*, dearie," smiled Rosie. "The crystal ball never lies. But it only speaks to them that 'as the gift."

"Oh, right," I said, trying not to smile. "Anyway, I'd better get back to the castle. Thanks again for catching Hercules."

"No worries!" said Jed. "We'll bring the kennel along later."

As soon as I was out of earshot I burst out laughing. The gift, indeed.

# Chapter Five

## Battlement Brouhaha

As I approached the castle I saw half a dozen dummy guards up on the battlements. Patchcoat poked his head over the parapet and waved.

"What d'you think, Ced?" he called. "Just a few more to do."

I gave him the thumbs-up. "They look great!" I said. "I'll come up and give you a hand with the rest."

I climbed to the battlements and began to help Patchcoat. To my relief Hercules lay down in the late afternoon sun and dozed off with his head between his paws.

We had just dressed the final dummy in chain mail and plonked a helmet on its head when the door of the Great Hall opened below. A clean-shaven Sir Percy strode out into the courtyard. He was wearing his best tunic and a hat with a purple plume.

"Good gracious, Cedric!" he called, spotting the dummies. "Where did you get these men from? You know I can't afford to hire anyone. Dismiss them at once!"

"It's all right, Sir Percy," Patchcoat

laughed. "They're not real."

"Not real?"

Sir Percy climbed up to us. I got a whiff of his pungent new aftershave as he turned to stroll along the front battlements, inspecting the dummy guards.

Patchcoat waved his hand in front of his nose and screwed up his face. "Phwoar!" he whispered. "Talk about a pong!"

Hercules woke with a start and looked around. He started to growl.

"Don't worry, boy," I said. "They're not actual soldiers. There's nothing to be scared of."

Sir Percy finished his inspection and turned to us. "Well, Cedric, I doubt if they'd fool *anyone* in daylight," he said, ignoring the fact that it was daylight now and they'd just totally fooled *him*. "But I suppose they're better than nothing."

*There's gratitude for you.*

Hercules suddenly sprang to his feet, barking furiously.

"I say, what an awful racket," said Sir Percy. "Do make him stop, Cedric."

I tried soothing Hercules, but it was no use.

"Sorry, Sir Percy," I said, gripping the dog's lead. "I think he's a bit spooked by the dummies."

"Well, really!" my master said. "Silly animal. Cedric, let him come to me. *I'll* calm him down for you."

"Are you sure, Sir Percy?" I said doubtfully.

"Of course, dear boy," Sir Percy said breezily. "A dog instinctively understands the, er, *natural authority* of its master. Namely myself. All it requires is a firm hand and a stern tone. Untie his lead."

"Yes, Sir Percy."

"Hold on, Ced," Patchcoat piped up, as I started to undo the lead. "Are you *sure* Herc's bothered by the dummies? I mean, he didn't bark at them earlier, when you first came back from the woods."

"Hmm. Good point," I said. "You don't think—?"

"Cedric! What are you waiting for?" Sir Percy interrupted. He whistled and clapped his hands. "Here, boy!"

"Er, Sir Percy, I think I'd better hold on—"

But it was too late. With an extra loud WOOF! Hercules tore himself from my grip and hurtled along the battlements towards Sir Percy.

"You see how he obeys his master?" beamed Sir Percy. "Now watch and learn, Cedric." He fixed the pooch with a stern stare, pointed at the ground and ordered, "Sit!"

But Hercules didn't sit. He didn't stop either. He just bared his fangs, snarled and kept on running.

"Uh-oh," said Patchcoat. "It's not the dummies he's after, Ced. It's Sir Percy!"

A few seconds earlier my master had looked rather smug. Now he looked distinctly alarmed.

"Stop! Sit! Sit, I say!" he quavered. "Cedric! Call him off at once! Aargh!"

# KNIGHTMARE

"Hercules! Bad dog!" I cried, but it was no use.

Sir Percy turned and fled along the battlements, with Hercules snapping at the seat of his best tunic. Patchcoat and I set off in hot pursuit, trying to get close enough to grab the dog's collar.

# KNIGHTMARE

We had just run a complete lap of the battlements when we heard the sound of hooves and wheels rumbling up to the gate.

"The baron!" cried Sir Percy. "He's early. That's all I need!"

In his panic Sir Percy failed to see a spare battleaxe lying on the ground.

"Sir Percy!" I yelled. "Watch out!"

Too late. Sir Percy tripped on the battleaxe, careered sideways and collided with the parapet with such force that his hat flew off and dropped into the moat below. He managed to right himself – but then Hercules caught up with him.

SNARL! SNAP!

"OOCHYA! OW!"

I winced as the
dog pounced and
sank his fangs
into my master's
bottom. There was
a ripping sound
as Sir Percy leaped
into the air in shock, lost his
balance – and tipped over the battlements!

Patchcoat and I dashed forward
and seized Sir Percy's legs just in time.
A moment later and he'd have plunged
headfirst into the castle moat.

"Help!" he screeched from inside the
skirts of his tunic, which had flopped over
his head. "Get me up!"

This turned out to be easier said than done. My master was just too heavy. Not only that, but Hercules had his paws up on the parapet, ready to take another chomp of Sir Percy's posterior as soon as we'd hauled it within reach.

"We're – trying – Sir – Percy!" I puffed.

"Hey! You chaps need a hand up there?"

I looked down to see Jed and Rosie jumping from their caravan. It was them we'd heard arriving.

"Yes please!" I called. "But hurry! We can't hold him much longer!"

"My boots!" Sir Percy wailed. "They're slipping off. Help!"

Jed and Rosie sped to the gate and

# KNIGHTMARE

appeared on the battlements beside us
moments later. Rosie pulled Hercules away
while Jed reached a muscular arm over the
parapet, grabbed Sir Percy by the seat of
his pants and yanked him back to safety.

"There you go, Your Honour!" said Jed.

My master cringed feebly at Hercules, who growled back at him. Rosie restrained the dog, while I tied his lead firmly to his collar.

"I've no idea who you two people are," groaned Sir Percy. "But just keep that disobedient brute away from me!"

"Brute? What, him?" said Jed. "But he's as sweet as pie, Your Honour." He ruffled Hercules's fur. The dog instantly jumped up to give him a good licking. "Hey, boy!" he chuckled. "Less o' that. I had a wash this mornin'. Sit!"

Hercules sat at once, his tail thumping the ground.

"Impressive!" I said.

"He's a monster!" huffed Sir Percy. "Cedric, what on earth possessed you to bring home that beast?"

*Um – YOU did, Sir Percy*, I thought. But I just said, "Sorry, Sir Percy."

"From now on I don't want it anywhere near me. It can jolly well sleep outside the castle."

"Yes, Sir Percy."

"Well, at least he'll have a nice place to sleep," said Jed. "I've made that kennel."

"Where shall we put it, Your Honour?" said Rosie.

"*You* decide, Cedric," said Sir Percy. "I've had quite enough of dogs for one day.

83

I'm going to change my tunic."

With a nervous glance at Hercules, Sir Percy staggered down to the courtyard and back into the castle. Rosie stared after him.

"Now there's a funny thing, Master Cedric," she said. "I know I've seen Sir Percy before. But I can't think where."

"At the May Fair?" I suggested.

"Hmm. Not sure, dearie," she said. "Maybe it was in me crystal ball—"

"Come on, Rosie," Jed interrupted. "Let's unload this kennel."

We followed Jed and Rosie to the caravan. Strapped to the back was a large kennel, skilfully made out of sturdy logs.

Together we carried it to a spot near the

drawbridge. Hercules dived inside at once
with a contented WOOF!

"Right, we'll be off," said Jed. "It's
almost sunset and we might not find our
camp after dark. Bye!"

"Bye. And thanks for making the kennel
so quickly," I said.

Patchcoat and I watched the caravan
trundle off.

"Well, Hercules certainly likes his new
home," I said. The dog was already dozing
in his kennel, his head on his front paws.
"Perhaps he's a bit too cosy in there. He
doesn't exactly fit the image of a fierce
guard dog. He looks like he wouldn't hurt
a fly!"

"Except for Sir Percy," Patchcoat said.

"Yes, I wonder what that was all about?"

But before Patchcoat could reply, we heard the sound of a trumpet.

ROOT-I-TOOT-I-TOOT!

It was coming from about half a mile away on the edge of the woods. There was another sound, too, like a heavy cart crunching over the ground.

"Uh-oh," I said. "That's definitely the baron this time. We'd better turn ourselves into guards!"

"Too right," said Patchcoat. "I'd forgotten about that."

We dashed to the battlements, where we'd left the spare gear from the cellar. A few minutes later I was dressed in a baggy adult-size mailcoat, a slightly mildewed surcoat and an oversized helmet that hid half my face. We grabbed a battleaxe each and hurried back to the gate to see Baron Fitztightly riding up at the head of a company of marching soldiers led by a sergeant. But it wasn't the troops that caught my eye. It was what they were escorting. Clattering along on giant wheels, pulled by two enormous carthorses, was the biggest catapult I had ever seen.

# Chapter Six

## Catapult Chaos

"Company – HALT!" bellowed the sergeant, as the convoy reached the drawbridge. "Atten-*SHUN*!"

The baron rode across the drawbridge to the gate.

"You there!" he said to me and Patchcoat. "We're here on the king's business. Where's your master?"

# KNIGHTMARE

"Er…" I began. Good question.

Luckily, Sir Percy came scuttling across the courtyard at that very moment, hastily pulling a fresh hat on to his head. It was the wrong way round.

# KNIGHTMARE

"Ah, there you are, Sir Percy," said the baron.

"Greetings, my lord!" said Sir Percy. "I say, jolly nice battering ram you've got there. The king *will* be pleased!"

"Trebuchet," corrected the baron.

"Bless you!" said Sir Percy.

"What?" snapped the baron. "Sir Percy, *this* is a trebuchet. It's a type of siege catapult. I thought you'd know that, considering all the cities you've captured," he added, raising an eyebrow. "According to *The Song of Percy*."

That's the title of my master's book. It's very popular. And also very, ahem, *imaginative*.

# KNIGHTMARE

"Oh! Ah! Of course I knew that!" said my master. "It was just my, er, little joke, my lord. Ha, ha, ha!"

The baron frowned. "The Castlecruncher is the most powerful catapult in the kingdom," he said. "It can fling a one-ton rock nearly half a mile. Demolish a whole castle in no time. It would be a *disaster* if it fell into the hands of one of the king's enemies. Like Snorbert the Sneaky."

King Snorbert was the ruler of Lumbago, one of the neighbouring kingdoms.

"On the way here I received an urgent despatch from the king," the baron went on. "Our spies in Lumbago believe that Snorbert has sent a couple of *his* spies to try and steal the catapult. We can't let that happen."

"Don't worry, baron," said Sir Percy. "It'll be as safe as houses here at Castle Bombast!"

"Good," said the baron. He turned to the soldiers. "Right, men, bring it into the castle!"

Guided by the sergeant, the carthorses started to haul the catapult across the drawbridge. But the horses had only gone a little way when they stopped.

"What's the matter, sergeant?" said the baron.

"Sorry, sir," said the sergeant. "No room, sir."

It was true. The swinging-arm was too tall to get through the gate of the castle.

"Oh, *brilliant*," tutted the baron. "I knew we should have stopped at a bigger castle, but His Majesty assured me this was the safest place in the kingdom."

"Oh it is, baron, it is!" said Sir Percy.

"It had better be," said the baron. "We shall have to leave the catapult outside the castle. My soldiers need a good night's rest, so I'm relying on *your* lot to protect the trebuchet, Sir Percy. I hope they're up to the job."

"Oh yes!" said Sir Percy. "My very best guards will be on sentry duty all night."

"Glad to hear it," the baron said,

looking around. "Where are they?"

"Ah, *here*, my lord," said Sir Percy. He
nodded at me and Patchcoat.

The baron raised an eyebrow. "Your
*very best* guards?" he said. "Really?"

Sir Percy hastily pointed upwards. "And
I also have, er, a crack platoon patrolling
the battlements."

# KNIGHTMARE

Baron Fitztightly peered up at the dummy guards. Luckily it was now early evening and the light was fading.

"Hmm," he said doubtfully. "They don't look like they're doing much patrolling to me, Sir Percy."

"Oh, and I have a highly trained guard dog," said Sir Percy, who was obviously keen for the baron to stop staring at the battlements. "It lives in that kennel at the end of the drawbridge. Savage beast. Very rare breed, you know."

"The kennel appears to be *empty*, Sir Percy."

Yikes! In the panic to go and change into our guards' outfits, I'd forgotten to tie

# KNIGHTMARE

Hercules up. We'd just left him dozing in the kennel. But where was he now?

It didn't take long to find out.

There was a shriek from inside the castle. Then the kitchen door flew open and Hercules came hurtling out with a plucked starling in his mouth and a furious Margaret in hot pursuit.

"Come back 'ere, you mangy mutt!"

With a yelp of terror, Sir Percy dived behind the baron for safety as Hercules bounded towards us. I ran forward and managed to grab his lead – which wasn't easy with a heavy battleaxe in one hand and a wobbly helmet falling over my eyes.

"Bad dog!" I said, as Margaret snatched the scraggy (and rather chewed) bird from Hercules's slobbery jaws.

"First he snaffles all me leftover giblets, then he nicks one o' me starlings," she puffed. "If I catch that fleabag in the kitchen again, the next stew I make will taste of *dog*!"

She turned and stumped back inside, wiping the starling on her apron. I led Hercules away and tied him firmly to the chain of the castle drawbridge.

"*Highly trained*, eh?" sighed the baron wearily. "Sir Percy, kindly show me to my quarters. Your squire can bring my bag."

"Er, my *squire*?" said Sir Percy. "Ah, yes. Right. My squire. Yes." He turned to me and gave one of his embarrassingly obvious winks. "I say, you there, guard chappie! Run and tell Master Cedric to bring up the baron's luggage, would you? Hurry now! Chop-chop!"

"Yessir," I said, putting on a deep voice. "I mean, no, sir."

# KNIGHTMARE

I ran into the courtyard and ducked into
the stables. I swiftly pulled off my helmet
and chain mail, then ran back to fetch
the baron's overnight bag from his saddle.
As I delivered it to his room, Sir Percy was
telling the baron about the "exotic cuisine"
Margaret was preparing for dinner. That
reminded me that Patchcoat and I hadn't
eaten either. There would be no chance once
we were outside on guard duty, so I nipped
down to the kitchen and popped some bread
and a big lump of cheese into a cloth when
Margaret had her back turned.

After that I stabled the baron's horse,
then took some hay to the carthorses. There
wasn't room for them in the stables so

they'd also be spending the night outside, tethered to the catapult. The sergeant was sitting on the edge of it with his boot off, rubbing a dock leaf on a blister.

"You and your men are sleeping in the – um – *lower wing* of the castle." I said. "It's not very luxurious, but better than sleeping outdoors. The cook will give you something to eat once the baron and Sir Percy have had dinner."

"Thanks, sonny," said the sergeant, pulling his boot back on. "Hold on, though. We can't leave the catapult guarded by one measly sentry." He nodded at Patchcoat, who was still at his post by the gate, cracking jokes with the soldiers.

"Looks likes that other fellow has skived off somewhere!"

"I'll go and fetch him," I said. "I've got a good idea where he is."

I nipped back to the stables, pulled on my guard's outfit and returned to the gate.

"There you are," said the sergeant. "Good. Now, where's that squire? He was going to show us to our billet."

"Oh, he, er, had to run an errand for his master," I said in my deep voice. "The door to your billet is next to the kitchen."

"Right, lads!" barked the sergeant. "Fall in! By the left, quick, MARCH! Left, right, left right…"

They filed off into the castle.

# KNIGHTMARE

"Phew!" said Patchcoat. "So far so good, Ced."

"Just about," I replied. "Come on, let's shut up shop."

I closed the castle gates. Then, after checking that Hercules was safely installed in his kennel, we settled down for a night on guard.

# Chapter Seven

## Nighttime Knockout

A few hours later, the castle was quiet. The baron and the troops had all eaten and gone to bed. Patchcoat and I planned to take it in turns to sleep, but soon abandoned that idea. There was no chance of either of us dozing off. Not with Hercules snoring so loudly. And that wasn't the only sound coming from the kennel. I blame

# KNIGHTMARE

Margaret's leftover giblets. If the noise hadn't kept us awake, the whiff certainly would have done.

We'd taken off our helmets and were sitting against the catapult, scoffing our scrounged supper, when something caught my eye. A small flicker of light, over in the woods. A second later it had disappeared. Patchcoat had seen it, too.

"That'll be Rosie and Jed," he said. "Looks like they've got a campfire."

"But campfires don't just *vanish*," I said. "It was like a torch going out."

"I wouldn't worry," said Patchcoat. "It's probably just poachers."

"Oh yes," I said. "I spotted some in the

woods earlier. I forgot to tell Sir Percy."

"Poachers," grinned Patchcoat. "Or maybe … King Snorbert's *spies* sneaking up on the castle, eh, Ced?"

"Very funny," I shivered. "I'd rather not think about spies, thanks very much."

"Only kidding," said Patchcoat. "Even if it was a couple of spies, they'd never be able to sneak off with this giant catapult. And even if they tried, we'd raise the alarm as soon as we saw them coming."

I yawned. "You're right," I said. "Something tells me this is going to be a long, boring night. I'll just have a quick stretch of my legs to wake myself up."

I walked over to the moat. In the

moonlight I spotted something floating
by the edge of the water. I bent down
for a closer look and realized it was Sir
Percy's hat. Just as I fished it out, I heard
Patchcoat behind me, so I turned and said,
"Look what I've found!"

But it wasn't Patchcoat. It was a stranger,
wrapped in a scarf and wearing a broad-
brimmed hat. He looked vaguely familiar.

"Oh," I said. "Who are you?"

And then something bashed me on the head and everything went dark.

I opened my eyes and blinked. I was lying on my back, staring at the stars. My head was throbbing. After a few seconds I remembered. The stranger in front of me. The clonk on the head from behind. The moon was much lower in the sky, so I guessed I'd been out cold for at least a couple of hours. It had to be after midnight.

I heard a grunt nearby and sat up. Over by the drawbridge I could make out Patchcoat getting to his knees. I stood up and staggered over to him.

"What happened?" he groaned, rubbing the back of his head.

"Looks like we were knocked unconscious," I said.

"I'd sort of worked *that* bit out," Patchcoat said. "But who did it?"

"Poachers?"

"Unlikely. Poachers wouldn't come so close to the castle," said Patchcoat.

"Who, then?" I wondered. "Hey, do you think it was the spies?"

"Dunno, Ced. One thing's for sure, though. Hercules ain't gonna win any prizes for being a guard dog!"

It was true. Hercules was still snoring

away in his kennel. I frowned as he let out a loud PARP.

"Something's not right," I said.

"You're telling me!" said Patchcoat, holding his nose. "Pooh!"

"No, not that," I said. "Maybe my head's still a bit fuzzy. But I've got a feeling that something's ... missing."

"Our helmets?" said Patchcoat. "We took them off, remember? When we were eating, over by the catap— Oh."

I followed Patchcoat's gaze and gasped.

The catapult wasn't there. And nor were the carthorses.

Suddenly we heard the front gate open. We just had time to plonk our helmets back on when the sergeant appeared with one of his men.

"Thought we'd give you chaps a break," said the sergeant. "'Ere! Where's the catapult?"

"WHAT!" bawled the baron, as he stood at the end of the drawbridge in his dressing gown. "A whole blithering catapult and two carthorses, stolen from under your noses?"

"S-somebody knocked us out, sir," I explained. "There were at least two people. I caught a glimpse of one of them before I was hit."

"I see," said the baron. "But it doesn't

explain why your fellow guards up there on the battlements didn't notice what was happening and come to your aid," he seethed. "And what about that guard dog? Why didn't it bark?"

He indicated Hercules, who had finally woken up amid all the kerfuffle. I was holding him tightly by his lead to stop him jumping up and giving the baron a friendly licking.

"I don't know, sir," I fibbed. The correct answer, of course, was *because he's the most useless guard dog in the kingdom.* But I figured it wouldn't be too helpful to say that.

The baron turned to the sergeant.

"Sergeant, head up the road with half a dozen men," he said. "A huge lumbering thing like a catapult can't have got far. After all, it's not like stealing a box of jewels. You can hardly hide it under your tunic. With a bit of luck you'll soon catch up with those enemy spies."

"Yessir!" The sergeant saluted and hurried off.

The baron called after him. "Oh, and

send one of your men to fetch those short-sighted dimwits from the battlements," he ordered. "I want to know exactly why they failed to spot a two-ton catapult being hauled away in broad moonlight!"

"Yessir!"

Uh-oh. The baron was already furious. Something told me he was about to get a whole lot angrier.

"There's something else that bothers me," the baron said, once the sergeant and a squad of royal troops had jogged off down the road. "I'm surprised no one heard the catapult being stolen, even if they managed not to see it."

Patchcoat and I exchanged glances.

# KNIGHTMARE

The baron was right. It *was* rather odd. The wheels and the horses' hooves must have made a heck of a racket. Even somebody *inside* the castle would have heard it, never mind outside.

Just then a soldier came out of the gate carrying a torch. The baron had sent him to fetch Sir Percy. Sure enough, my master was traipsing behind him in his nightgown, bleary-eyed and still half-asleep. Hercules started to growl.

"Sir Percy!" snapped the baron. "At last!"

"Do you have any idea what time it is?" Sir Percy grumbled, keeping a wary eye on the dog. He pointed at the soldier.

"This chap had better have a jolly good reason for getting me out of bed in the middle of the ni—"

"Oh, stop fussing, man!" yelled the baron. "The catapult has been stolen!"

My master's jaw dropped open. "Eh? Who? H-how?" he babbled. He turned to me. "Is this true, Cedric?"

Too late, he realized his mistake. Staring at me in astonishment, the baron stepped forward and plucked off my helmet.

"That's torn it," sighed Patchcoat. He took off his own helmet. Now Sir Percy had blown my cover, there was no more point in pretending.

"Squire Cedric!" gasped the baron. "And that jester fellow! Sir Percy, what the DEUCE is going on?"

Before Sir Percy could reply, another soldier came running out of the castle.

"Yer Lordship!" he panted, saluting. "I went to fetch the guards from the battlements like the sergeant said and—"

Sir Percy's eyes widened in alarm.

"Can't you see I'm busy, soldier?" interrupted the baron. "Right, Sir Percy. I want to ask your men how each and every one of them failed to spot a catapult being stolen by the king's enemies."

"But ... but ... Yer Lordship," said the soldier. "Those guards – they ain't real!"

"Eh? What on earth do you mean?" spluttered the baron. "What are they then? Monkeys?"

"They're *dummies*, Yer Lordship! Every one o' them!"

The baron was speechless. He was clearly having trouble taking it all in.

"*Wh-what?*" he spluttered. "Are you telling me those spies have kidnapped

# KNIGHTMARE

Sir Percy's guards and replaced them with *dummies?*"

And then a look came over his face. The look of someone who had just heard a very large penny dropping. Shaking with rage, the baron fixed Sir Percy with a long, hard stare.

"So *that's* it," he thundered. "His Majesty's new weapon has fallen into the hands of King Snorbert and it's all YOUR fault, Sir Percy! You told the king that Castle Bombast was the strongest castle in the kingdom. That's why we brought the catapult here. But that was just one of your stupid boasts, wasn't it? We might as well have taken it straight to Lumbago and given it to King Snorbert as a present! Have you any idea how FURIOUS the king will be? You, Sir Percy, are in BIG trouble!"

"Ah, well, my dear baron," burbled my master. "I, er – um – I can explain. It's – um – it's like this, you see. When I wrote to the king I, er, I had a full battalion of guards. Honestly! But then, just yesterday, alas, they all – um – um – came down with a dose of – of, er, let's just call it a rather *explosive* ailment."

"*What?*" said the baron. "Are you *serious*, Sir Percy?"

"Oh yes, indeed, my lord!" said my master, now well warmed up for a barefaced fib fest. "Awful it was!

The stench! Poor blighters. I had to, er, send them all off home. Couldn't have Your Lordship or the king's troops catching the tummy trots, could I? And then – and then – I ordered my *squire* here to pop down the road to Sir Spencer's place and – um – er, ask him if I could borrow some of his guards."

The porky pie was so outrageous I could hardly stop myself from gasping.

"Well, Sir Percy?" said the baron suspiciously. "Why didn't you?"

"Ah well, you see, Cedric here had this *ridiculous* idea of using dummies instead. To – um – save time. I fear I went along with it. Foolish, I know, but – but—"

# KNIGHTMARE

"Enough!" barked the baron. "Sir Percy, do you *seriously* expect me to believe such a barrel of nonsense? Blaming your poor squire indeed! Oh, when the king hears of this—"

Sir Percy dived forward and clasped the baron's knees. "Anything but that!" he wailed. "Don't tell the king! I won't do it again! I promise! Just PLEASE don't tell the king!"

# KNIGHTMARE

My master's pathetic grovelling was interrupted by the sound of marching feet. We turned to see the sergeant and his men returning up the road.

"Sorry, Your Lordship," the sergeant said. "We didn't find the catapult. But we did find a couple o' suspicious foreigners in the woods. They was creepin' about near the road. Bring 'em up, lads!"

The soldiers marched towards the castle leading a pair of prisoners with their hands tied. Patchcoat and I exchanged horrified looks. It was Jed and Rosie!

# Chapter Eight
## Tracker Cracker

"It was nothing to do with us, Yer Honours!" said Jed.

"Master Cedric will vouch for us, won't you?" pleaded Rosie.

"That's right!" I said. "Please let them go. They're just harmless travelling folk."

"Is that so?" said the baron. "Then what were they doing sneaking around at night?"

# KNIGHTMARE

"Um – well…" Jed looked rather sheepish. "Catchin' rabbits, Yer Honour."

"Sorry, Master Cedric," said Rosie. "We ain't poachers, honest. We was 'ungry, that's all."

"Rabbits?" said the sergeant. "Rubbish. How do you explain this?" He fished in his tunic and pulled out a silver coin. "We found it in his pocket, Your Lordship. He claims he was given it to pay for a kennel!"

"It's true!" I piped up. "I found the coin in the woods just before I met Jed and Rosie here. Someone had dropped it. We thought it was probably poachers."

"*Poachers*, indeed," snorted the sergeant. "Take a look, Your Lordship."

# KNIGHTMARE

The baron held the coin up to the torchlight. "A foreign coin bearing the head of … King Snorbert! Master Cedric, I fear these gypsies have duped you. Where did you pick up this coin? Near their camp?"

# KNIGHTMARE

"Well, yes, my lord, but…"

"Aha. There you are then," said the baron. "One of the gypsies probably dropped it themselves, and you just happened to find it."

"That ain't true!" cried Jed

"Silence!" said the baron. "Sergeant, lock them up. I shall deal with them later. This castle *does* at least have a *dungeon*, doesn't it, Sir Percy?"

Sir Percy had been trying to slip into the shadows while the baron's back was turned. He froze in his tracks.

"Eh? Ah! A dungeon? Yes, of course, Your Lordship," he said.

"Good," said the baron. "Sergeant, take

the gypsies away."

"But I'm sure they had nothing to do with it, Your Lordship!" I piped up, as Jed and Rosie were led off. "The man I saw by the moat was definitely a lot taller than them."

"But you didn't see his *accomplice*, did you, Master Cedric? Whoever it was that knocked you out," said the baron. "Now, kindly saddle my horse."

"Yes, Your Lordship," I said. There seemed little point in arguing. For one thing, squires are NOT allowed to argue with a lord. And for another, I had no actual proof that Jed and Rosie were innocent.

"And saddle Sir Percy's, too."

# KNIGHTMARE

"Eh? What?" said my master. "Who, me?"

"Yes, *you*, Sir Percy," said the baron. "This mess is *entirely* your fault," he went on. "You and I will ride fast and see if we can catch up with the catapult. If there are only two or three spies, we should be able to handle them."

"Um – you mean do some *fighting*, Your Lordship?" Even in the torchlight, I could see Sir Percy go pale.

"Of course. So bring your sword. We may be outnumbered, but we'll do our best."

"But … but what about my armour?" Sir Percy quailed.

"No time for that, man!" said the baron.

"We must leave at once. I'm giving you one chance, Sir Percy. If we recapture the catapult, I *might* pretend that this whole sorry episode never happened. But make no mistake, if we fail, I shall be taking *three* prisoners back to the palace. And I'll recommend to the king that he locks you in the royal dungeons for a good long stretch!"

Leaving Hercules with Patchcoat for a moment, I quickly saddled the baron's horse and Prancelot, Sir Percy's horse. She was very unhappy at being woken. But not half as unhappy as Sir Percy looked, riding off into the night to face King Snorbert's spies.

Patchcoat and I stood near the moat and watched them head down the road that ran through the woods. We'd pulled off our chain mail, which was a relief. (It was heavy and scratchy.)

"I wish we could do something," I said. "I'm still sure Jed and Rosie have nothing to do with this."

"I know," said Patchcoat. "It doesn't make sense, Ced. If they *were* involved, why would they stay in the woods? Why not escape with the others?"

Hercules had been sniffing the air. He suddenly started tugging on his lead.

"Looks like he's spotted something," I said, peering in the moonlight. "Over there, on the ground."

It was a hat. Patchcoat picked it up and handed it to me.

"Is it the one Sir Percy dropped in the moat?"

# KNIGHTMARE

I held it up. "No," I said. It looked familiar though. "I'm sure it's the one that stranger was wearing! He must've dropped it in the dark."

Patchcoat smiled as Hercules barked happily. "I think he wants to give it a good chewing!"

"Hmm," I said. "I wonder. It's worth a try…"

I held the hat to Hercules's nose, just far away enough so he could get a good sniff without grabbing it.

Then I walked a few paces away, closer to the moat. "Right, boy," I said. "Fetch!"

I swung my arm as if I was about to spin the hat a long way, like a throwing disc. But at the last minute, I whipped the hat behind my back and tossed it in the water.

"Where's it gone, eh?" I said, stepping forward again. "Look for it! Good boy!"

To begin with Hercules wandered around sniffing the air, trying in vain to find the hat. Just when I thought he'd given up, he suddenly put his nose to the ground and pulled me in the direction of the road.

"Brilliant!" I said. "If I'm right, he's picked up the scent of the person who dropped the hat! With a bit of luck we'll

find out which way the spies headed after
they left the castle."

"Good one, Ced," beamed Patchcoat.
"Maybe this mutt isn't so dumb after all."

Sure enough, Hercules led us up the
road, away from the castle. Before long we
were passing through Sir Percy's woods. But
then he suddenly veered off to the right,
down an old track into the trees.

"Bother," I said. "I think he's lost the
scent. He's probably gone after a rabbit."

"No he hasn't, Ced," said Patchcoat.
"Look!"

He pointed to a muddy patch of track in
front of us. In the moonlight we could make
out hoofprints and the wheel ruts left by the

catapult. The prints and ruts were a bit fuzzy, which was odd. But the freshly trampled grass told us they were definitely new.

We followed the track to a clearing. In the middle stood the gypsy caravan.

"Oh dear," I said. "Perhaps Jed and Rosie *were* mixed up in this after all."

"I wouldn't be so sure," said Patchcoat. "Hercules isn't going near the caravan."

It was true. Hercules pulled us away from the clearing and on through the woods. The way grew less distinct, the trees started to thin out and before long we found ourselves at the entrance to a rocky, overgrown hollow. It seemed to be an old quarry.

"Looks like the end of the road," I said. "Hercules must've been leading us on a wild goose chase after all."

"Shh!" said Patchcoat suddenly.

Voices. Up ahead. And a flicker of light.

"Let's sneak up and listen," I said. "But we'd better leave Hercules here in case he makes a noise."

I tied Hercules to a tree. Then Patchcoat and I slipped into the hollow and crept silently up to a cluster of mossy boulders. Peeping through a gap, I saw two men wrapped in blankets, lying by a campfire beside a huge overhanging rock. Nearby stood a cart with a name on the side: *Ralph's Rugs.*

"Drat," I muttered. "We've been wasting our time."

After all that, Hercules had only led us to the two merchants I'd passed on the road to Stoke Bluster the day before.

Patchcoat scrambled a bit higher to get a better view. I was about to tell him not to bother when he suddenly hissed, "Blimey!"

I clambered up to join him. My jaw dropped open. I could see not only the merchants and their cart, but also two large carthorses tethered to a tree. And that wasn't all.

"Good old Hercules!" grinned Patchcoat.

Tucked inside the overhanging rock was the catapult.

## Chapter Nine
## Tunnel Tumult

Patchcoat and I edged a bit closer to the fire to hear what the "merchants" were saying.

"So, Nastikoff, let's get this straight," said one. "We camp out here for a few days until the fuss has died down a bit."

"Correct, Skowl," said the other. I noticed he had no hat on. "King Fredbert's men will assume we're making straight for Lumbago. They'll check every road and border crossing, but there'll be no sign of us. In a few days they'll just think we've given them the slip. I'd love to see the look on Fredbert's face. He'll be *so* cross!"

The two men fell about laughing.

"Meanwhile, we dismantle the catapult," said the one named Skowl. "Then, when things are quieter, we smuggle it out of the country bit by bit."

"Correct again," said Nastikoff. "In the cart, hidden under rugs and blankets. I reckon we should do it in about three or four trips. No one will pay any attention to a couple of travelling rug merchants."

"Oh, King Snorbert will be so pleased!" Skowl smirked. "He'll probably give us both the Order of the Snoop!"

"Not if we can help it," I whispered. "Come on, Patchcoat, let's get back to the castle!"

We slid down from the boulders and tiptoed back towards Hercules. But all we found was the chewed end of his lead, still tied around the tree.

"Oh no!" I said. *"Now* where's he gone?"

The answer came in the form of a large rat that came scuttling out of the bushes with Hercules in hot pursuit.

"EEEK!" I yelped, as rat and dog bounded away into the bushes again.

# KNIGHTMARE

"Come on, Ced," said Patchcoat. "I reckon they could've heard you shrieking back at Castle Bombast. We need to move sharpish."

Behind us came the sound of a cracking twig. Startled, we spun round to see the two spies. Their swords glinted in the moonlight.

"I'm afraid, gentlemen, you are too late," said Nastikoff.

"Consider yourselves prisoners of King Snorbert," sneered Skowl.

The spies frogmarched us under the overhang, where the catapult stood. From close up, we saw it had thick layers of rugs and blankets wrapped round each wheel. There were blankets on the horses'

hooves, too. So that was how they'd made such a quiet getaway. It also explained the fuzzy tracks the catapult had left in the woods.

"We will take you back to our country," said Nastikoff, taking a torch out of a crevice in the wall of the overhang. "And we will keep you there until your master pays for your release. You gentlemen have a wealthy master, yes?"

If only. We shook our heads.

"Pity," said Nastikoff. "But never mind. I'm sure you will both like living in one of our dungeons. For the rest of your lives."

The spies cackled unpleasantly.

"Now, gentlemen, I fear we must tie you up," said Skowl. He produced a coil of rope. "It is pointless to try to escape," he said. "But if you do it'll be worse for— Hey, what the—?"

The rat ran into the overhang, followed shortly afterward by Hercules, eagerly sniffing the ground as he tracked the rat's scent. He suddenly skidded to a halt and looked from me to Patchcoat to the strangers, as if wondering what was up.

I pointed at the spies and cried, "Get them, Hercules!"

WOOF! Before Skowl could move out of the way, Hercules pounced on him – and gave him a big friendly, slobbery lick. It wasn't quite what I'd meant, but it did the trick.

# KNIGHTMARE

Skowl staggered and nearly lost his balance, bumping into Nastikoff in the process. Nastikoff dropped the torch, which rolled in the dust and went out.

"Good boy, Hercules!" I cried. "Run for it, Patchcoat!"

But Nastikoff and Skowl were already scrambling to their feet, blocking our path.

"STOP!"

"Not bloomin' likely!" said Patchcoat.

"Quick, follow Hercules!" I said. The dog had picked up the rat's scent again and was running into the pitch darkness at the rear of the overhang. We only had a few seconds' head start, but I hoped it would be enough to lose the spies in the dark.

Then we could try and skirt around them
and run back outside.

At any moment I expected to hit a
wall of solid rock. But as Hercules's eager
snuffling got further and further ahead
of us, I realized the overhang went back
a lot further into the quarry face than I'd
thought. In fact, it seemed we were in some
kind of cave. I stretched my arms out wide
and felt cold stone on both sides.

"Funny cave, this," I said. "It feels like
it's the same width all the way along. And
the walls are incredibly smooth."

"So they are," said Patchcoat. "It's more
like a tunnel. Hmm. I wonder…"

At that moment there was a faint flicker

of light from behind us. The spies had obviously relit the torch.

"Surrender yourselves!" boomed Nastikoff. "You know you're trapped!"

"Yikes!" I said. "What shall we do?"

"Looks like we've got no choice," said Patchcoat. "Keep moving!"

We raced ahead, trying not to stumble in the dark, and with the odd gleam telling us that the spies were not far behind.

We'd been running for ages and my legs felt like they were about to drop off. Then I realized I was starting to run uphill.

"That's all I need!" I gasped.

At last the ground levelled out again.

"I don't know about you, Ced," panted

Patchcoat, "but do you think this tunnel is getting *wider*?"

Before I could answer there was a loud WOOF! and a pair of paws pinned me to the wall.

"Aargh! Hercules!" I squealed, trying to dodge his tongue. "I wondered where you'd got to."

The sound of running footsteps echoed behind us. I pushed the dog off me.

"Come on, we'd better keep going!"

"I hate to tell you this, Ced," said Patchcoat. "But there's no way out."

I held my hands out in front of me. After a few paces they met cold stone. I patted the wall all over, looking for a way through.

But Patchcoat was right. We'd come to a dead end.

Or had we? My hands touched something round and hard and metallic. Then it dawned on me. It was a door handle!

"Patchcoat!" I said. "There's a door! Quick, give me a hand!"

We tugged and heaved at the handle, but the door wouldn't budge.

"It's no good," said Patchcoat.

And then the spies appeared, out of breath. Both men were holding swords. Skowl had the coil of rope slung over one shoulder and a torch in his free hand. We could now see that we were in a small, dank chamber.

"We warned you it was useless to try to
escape!" Nastikoff snarled. "Hand me the
rope, Skowl."

Skowl gave the rope to Nastikoff, who
put down his sword while he uncoiled it.
Hercules sniffed the air and looked at
Nastikoff, his head cocked on one side.
Nastikoff hesitated.

"That dog," he grunted. "Why is it

staring at me? I don't like it."

"Oh, don't worry about that stupid mutt," said Skowl. "It's probably smelling another rat."

"*Two* rats, you mean," I said defiantly.

Nastikoff glared at me. "Why, you cheeky little—"

Without warning, Hercules gave a loud bark ... and pounced on Nastikoff.

"Aargh!" The spy lost his footing and toppled over backwards like a skittle. His head went CLONK against the wall and he sank to the floor with a groan.

"Nice work, Herc!" said Patchcoat.

With one spy out of action, we could probably have taken on Skowl. Except that he had a VERY sharp sword. And he didn't look afraid to use it.

"So, gentlemen," Skowl hissed. "There is no chance of escape. You may as well surrender."

We backed against the wall of the chamber. Skowl moved forwards, the blade of his sword flashing in the torchlight.

*Yikes*, I thought. *We're done for!*

SWISH!

Skowl swung his sword, but I ducked under the blade and dived for his knees. I clasped his legs together but he kicked me off and came at me again with the sword. This time Patchcoat ran at Skowl from the side and pushed him away, giving me a chance to get clear.

We now faced each other on opposite sides of the chamber. Skowl raised his sword once more.

"Interfering fools!" he growled. "You leave me with no choice."

He advanced towards us, a menacing sneer on his face.

And then the door burst open in an explosion of dust.

# Chapter Ten
## Slinger Surprise

As the dust began to settle we made out
a number of armed men standing in the
chamber. The chamber door lay on the
ground, wrenched off its hinges.

"Nobody move!" barked a familiar
voice.

"S-sergeant?" I said.

"Oh! It's you, Master Cedric," said the

sergeant. "We heard noises. Thought it was more of Snorbert's spies, come to help them gypsies escape. We forced the door."

"Yeah, we noticed," said Patchcoat.

"The gypsies are innocent," I said. "You're right about the spies, though. That's one of them over there." I pointed at Nastikoff. But there was no sign of Skowl. "Oh no! The other one must have escaped back down the tunnel. He's armed and dangerous!"

A faint whimpering came from under the door.

Patchcoat grinned. "Don't worry, Ced. I don't think he'll be giving us any more trouble."

"Look here," said the sergeant. "Can one of you explain what's been going on?"

I told him how Hercules's sniffing skills had led us to the catapult and the spies. "And then they chased us up the tunnel, and here we are," I said. "Which is where, exactly?"

The sergeant looked surprised.

"Why, don't you know?" he said. "You're in the cellars of Castle Bombast!"

"Thank goodness for that," said the baron. "If I'd returned to the palace without the catapult, His Majesty would have been *highly* displeased. And not only with *me*."

He gave Sir Percy a grim look.

"So, er, all's well that ends well, eh, my lord," my master said, with a fixed grin. "Now you've got the catapult back, you're going to – um – forget this happened? No harm done and all that?"

The baron nodded curtly. "Yes, I suppose so," he sighed. "If I told the king, he'd lock you in the royal dungeon – which, quite frankly, I think you deserve, Sir Percy.

# KNIGHTMARE

# KNIGHTMARE

But then Master Cedric and Master Patchcoat would be out of a job. And I wouldn't want that. If it wasn't for them we'd never have found the catapult."

"Actually it's Hercules you should thank, not us," I said.

We'd left Hercules in the kitchen, having a well earned feast of Margaret's leftovers.

"Good old Herc," said Patchcoat. "Not such a useless mutt after all, eh, Sir Percy?"

"Well, of course, I *knew* the dog had great potential," Sir Percy fibbed. "Which is why I *specifically* asked Cedric to buy an Egyptian terrier, er, thingummy-whatsit. Isn't that so, Cedric?"

A squire must never contradict his

master, so I had no choice but to grit my teeth and answer, "Yes, Sir Percy."

It was early morning and we were standing by the road that led through the wood. The convoy was preparing to leave with the catapult, which the sergeant and his men had retrieved from the spies' hideout. Nastikoff and Skowl were tied up on the back of their own cart, with a couple of the king's soldiers for company.

"Those spies should count themselves lucky," said the baron. "I've a jolly good mind to make them walk."

He turned to Jed and Rosie, who were watching with us at the side of the road. "My apologies for locking you up," he said.

# KNIGHTMARE

"Master Cedric has explained everything."

"No problem, Your Honour," said Jed. "We all make mistakes, eh?"

I'd told the baron that when Hercules was following the spies' scent through the woods he'd totally ignored Jed and Rosie's caravan.

The baron pulled something shiny from his tunic and tossed it to Jed. The carpenter caught it neatly with one hand.

"The silver coin!" he said. "Are you sure, Your Honour?"

The baron smiled. "Of course," he said. "Besides, those spies won't be needing any money for a long, long time."

Rosie was staring at Sir Percy. Her face lit up. "It's him!" she said. "I knew I recognized him!"

"Eh?" said Jed. "What do you mean?"

"The flying man in me crystal ball, remember?"

I tried not to smile. "I hate to tell you this," I said. "But Sir Percy can't actually fly."

"Right, men, let's get moving!" the baron ordered.

"Good idea," said Sir Percy. "I need another shave. And a dab of my new aftershave. Has Your Lordship tried it? *Essence d'Anise* it's called. Rather expensive. French, I believe."

"Yes," said the baron. "It means 'aniseed essence'. It's for cooking. I fear you've been diddled, Sir Percy."

Aniseed? That rang a bell. I was trying to remember where I'd heard it. But my thoughts were interrupted by a cry from the direction of the castle.

"Stop that dog!"

We turned to see Hercules running towards us with something in his mouth. Once again Margaret was in pursuit.

"Blinkin' pooch!" she hollered. "First he cleans me out o' leftovers, then he grabs the special snail 'n' sparrow pie I was makin' for lunch!"

Patchcoat pulled a face. "Snail and sparrow? Nice work, Herc!"

Hercules slowed down to swallow the last of the pie. He sniffed the air. Then he spotted Sir Percy and started to growl.

And then I remembered. Aniseed. The one thing that drove Hercules mad!

"Ah. G-good doggy," Sir Percy stammered, backing against the catapult. "Nice doggy... Cedric, help!"

I tried to seize Hercules but he was too quick. He leaped at Sir Percy, who turned

# KNIGHTMARE

and scrambled up on to the catapult just in time to avoid another bite on the backside.

Hercules pounced again, and sank his teeth into my master's boot.

"Get him off!" Sir Percy cried, trying to tug his foot free. "Help! WAAAAH!"

Hercules had pulled Sir Percy's boot right off. Flailing wildly, my master shot forwards and tipped head over heels into the great leather sling of the catapult.

The soldiers were struggling not to giggle. The baron looked like he would burst.

At last I grabbed Hercules by the collar. "It's safe to come down now, Sir Percy," I said.

Sir Percy peered over the edge of the

sling and began to climb out. But he was finding it tricky, because the sling swayed like a giant hammock.

"Do you need a hand, Sir Percy?" I asked.

"I'm quite all right, thank you very much," said my master, with as much dignity as he could muster. "I'll just take hold of this stick."

"No!" the baron called suddenly. "Don't touch that! The mechanism's very delic—"

Too late. Sir Percy grabbed the stick.

CLICK!

"Watch out!"

SWISH – BOIIIIIING!

"WAAAAAAAAAAAAHHHHH!"

Everybody gasped as Sir Percy flew through the trees, over the castle grounds – and landed with a terrific SPLASH in the moat of Castle Bombast.

# KNIGHTMARE

"Are you all right, Sir Percy?" I called, as
I ran to help him out.

My master flopped on to the bank,
covered in slimy pondweed and stinking
mud. (The loos of Castle Bombast empty
straight into the moat. *Ew.*)

"C-Cedric," he muttered, hauling himself to his feet. "G-go and tell Margaret to boil a cauldron of water. I fear I shall need another bath. That's my second in two months!"

"Yes, Sir Percy," I said, trying not to laugh.

As I headed across the drawbridge into the castle, Rosie tapped me on the arm.

"You see, dearie," she chuckled. "The crystal ball never lies!"

PETER BENTLY

# KNIGHTMARE

## Life Stinks!

ROALD DAHL **WINNING AUTHOR** FUNNY PRIZE

Roland the Rotten has challenged my master, Sir Percy the Proud, to a JOUST. But Sir Percy doesn't want to fight – not even with his LUCKY UNDERPANTS on. So guess who's got to get him out of it? That's right. ME. (Hopefully with a bit of help from my friend, Patchcoat the Jester.)

There's going to be a **BANQUET** at Castle
Bombast. But it's not just any old banquet. The
king and queen will be attending, and they
expect the very best – or else! Which means
more work for **ME**. And I dread to think what
Sir Percy's **ARCH ENEMY**, Roland the Rotten,
will do when he finds out he's not invited.

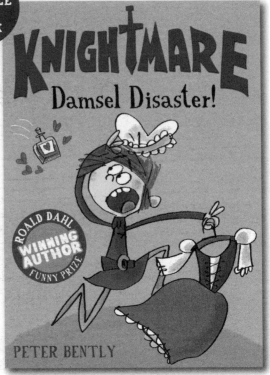

# KNIGHTMARE
## Damsel Disaster!

ROALD DAHL WINNING AUTHOR FUNNY PRIZE

PETER BENTLY

A **MEGA-RICH** princess is searching for a husband and Sir Percy thinks he's the knight for the job. So we're off to Noman Castle where there's going to be a test of **BRAVERY**. As usual, my master seems to have a **SNEAKY** plan up his sleeve. Ever seen a knight in a dress? Just so long as I don't have to wear one, too… Uh-oh!

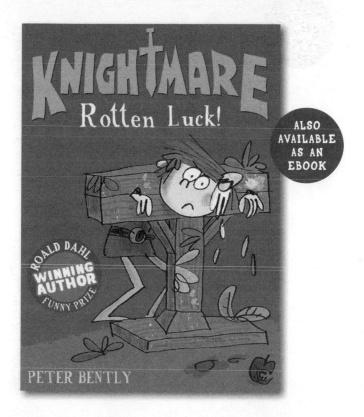

ALSO AVAILABLE AS AN EBOOK

ROALD DAHL WINNING AUTHOR FUNNY PRIZE

KNIGHTMARE
Rotten Luck!

PETER BENTLY

The Sheriff of Fleecingham is desperate
to capture a famous OUTLAW known as
the Ghost, and Sir Percy has accidentally
volunteered US for the job. But Grimwood
is dark and CREEPY. And I've heard there
are more than just robbers lurking in the
fearsome forest. Yikes! I'm not looking
forward to this mission one bit…

Sir Percy has been boasting again, and now
he has to WIN the football tournament at
the May Fair or he'll lose Castle Bombast!
Problem is, we haven't even got a TEAM.
Of course, it's up to ME to find some players.
But the only volunteers I can get have never
kicked a BALL in their lives...Eek!